Outings for the Mice of BRAMBLY HEDGE

JILL BARKLEM

Collins

An Imprint of HarperCollinsPublishers

This edition first published in Great Britain in 1999 by HarperCollins Publishers Ltd
This edition copyright © Jill Barklem 1999
Spring Story © Jill Barklem 1980
The High Hills © Jill Barklem 1986
ISBN 0 00 198 327 X
1 3 5 7 9 10 8 6 4 2

Printed in Singapore by Imago

SPRING STORY

It was the most beautiful morning. The spring sunshine crept into every cottage along Brambly Hedge and the little windows in the trees were opened wide.

All the mice were up early, but earliest of all was Wilfred, who lived with his family in the hornbeam tree. It was Wilfred's birthday.

Jumping out of bed, he ran into his parents' room and bounced on their bed till they gave him their presents.

"Happy birthday, Wilfred," said Mr and Mrs Toadflax sleepily.

He tore off the pretty wrappings and scattered them all over the floor. His squeaks of excitement woke his brother and sisters.

His parents turned over to go to sleep again. Wilfred went and sat on the stairs and blew his new whistle.

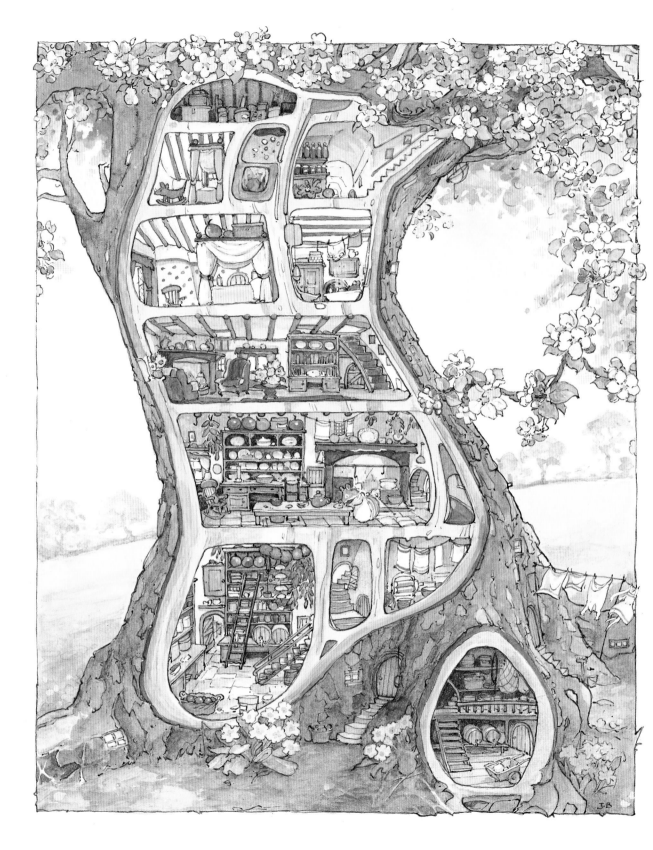

Mr and Mrs Apple lived next door at Crabapple Cottage. The sound of Wilfred's whistle floated in through their bedroom window. Mrs Apple got up and stretched. She sniffed the sweet air and went down to the kitchen to make a pot of elderflower tea. She was a very kindly mouse and a wonderful cook. The cottage always smelled of newly-made bread, fresh cakes and blackberry puddings.

"Breakfast's ready," she called. Mr Apple got out of bed with a sigh and joined her at the kitchen table. They ate their toast and jam and listened to Wilfred's warbling.

"I think somebody needs a lesson from the blackbird," said Mr Apple, brushing the crumbs from his whiskers and putting on his coat.

Mr Apple was a nice, old-fashioned sort of mouse. He was warden of the Store Stump where all the food for Brambly Hedge was kept.

The Store Stump was not far away. As Mr Apple
walked happily through the grass to the big front doors,
he felt someone pull his tail. He turned around quickly.
It was Wilfred, whistle in hand.

"It's my birthday!" he squeaked.

"Is it, young mouse," said Mr Apple. "Happy birthday
to you! Would you like to come and help me check the
Store Stump? We'll see what we can find."

In the middle of the Stump was an enormous hall, and leading off from it many passages and staircases. These led in turn to dozens of storerooms full of nuts and honey and jams and pickles. Each one had to be inspected. Wilfred's legs felt tired by the time they had finished and he sat by the fire in the hall to rest. Mr Apple lifted down a jar of sugared violets. He made a little cornet from a twist of paper and filled it with sweets. Taking Wilfred by the paw, he led him through the dark corridors out into the sun. Wilfred went to look for his brother and Mr Apple hurried down the hedge to visit his daughter Daisy and her husband, Lord Woodmouse.

Lord and Lady Woodmouse lived in the Old Oak Palace in the middle of the hedge. From the outside, the Palace looked like an ordinary oak tree, but inside the trunk was hollowed out to form a beautiful and many-roomed mansion.

At its heart was the grand ballroom. Polished doors led to magnificent kitchens, dining rooms, bedrooms, playrooms, spiral staircases and secret passages. Old Oak Palace had always been the home of the Woodmouse family.

Upstairs in the best bedroom, Lord and Lady Woodmouse woke to bright sunshine.

"What a perfect day!" sighed Lady Daisy as she nibbled a primrose biscuit. When they heard that Daisy's father had come to call, they were soon up and dressed and running down the winding stairs to greet him.

They found him in the kitchen drinking mint tea with Mrs Crustybread, the Palace cook. Daisy gave Mr Apple a kiss and sat down beside him.

"Hello Papa," she said. "What brings you here so early?"

"I've just met little Wilfred – it's his birthday today. Shall we arrange a surprise picnic for him?"

"What a wonderful idea," said Lord Woodmouse. Daisy nodded.

"I'll make him a special birthday cake if his mother agrees," said Mrs Crustybread, hurrying off to the pantry to find the ingredients.

Everyone was to be invited of course, so Mr Apple set off up the hedge towards the woods and Lord Woodmouse went down towards the stream calling at each house on the way.

The first house on Mr Apple's route was Elderberry Lodge. This fine elder bush was Basil's home. Basil was in charge of the Store Stump cellars. He was just getting up.

"A picnic eh? Splendid! I'll bring up some rose petal wine," he said, shuffling absent-mindedly round the room looking for his trousers. Basil had long white whiskers and always wore a scarlet waistcoat. He used to keep the other mice amused for hours with his stories.

"Ah, there you are, you rascals," he exclaimed, discovering his trousers behind the sofa.

Next Mr Apple came to the hornbeam. Mr Toadflax was sitting on his front doorstep eating bread and bramble jelly.

"We thought it would be nice to have a surprise picnic for your Wilfred," whispered Mr Apple. "We won't tell him what it's for and we'll all meet at midday by the Palace roots."

Mr Toadflax was delighted with the suggestion and went inside to tell his wife. Mr Apple went on to visit Old Vole who lived in a tussock of grass in the middle of the field.

Lord Woodmouse, meanwhile, was working his way down to the stream. The news had travelled ahead of him and all along the hedge excited mice leaned out of their windows to ask when the picnic would take place.

"I'll see if I can find some preserves," said old Mrs Eyebright.

"Shall we bring tablecloths?" called the weavers
who lived in the tangly hawthorn trees.

Poppy Eyebright from
the dairy promised cheeses,

and Dusty Dogwood, the Miller,
offered a batch of buns.

Mice soon began calling at the Store Stump to collect clover flour and honey, bramble brandy and poppy seeds, and all the other good things needed for the picnic. Mrs Crustybread baked a huge hazelnut cake with layers of thick cream and Wilfred's mother decorated it. Mrs Apple made some of her special primrose puddings.

Wilfred knew that there was to be an outing and that if he behaved, he would be allowed to go. He did his best but with a new whistle, a drum and a peashooter for his birthday, it wasn't easy.

When the Toadflax family arrived at the Palace,
Wilfred was rather disappointed that no one there
seemed to know that it was his birthday. Indeed he
had rather hoped for a few more presents, but it

would have been rude to drop hints, so he hid
his feelings as best he could. At a signal from
Lord Woodmouse they all set off with their baskets,
hampers and wheelbarrows.

Everyone had something to carry. Wilfred was given an
enormous basket, so heavy he could hardly lift it. Mr Apple
lent him a wheelbarrow, and his brother and sisters helped
him to push it, but still poor Wilfred found it hard to keep up.

It was a very long way. Heaving and pulling, wheeling and hauling, the mice made their way round the Palace, through the cornfield and up by the stream. Wilfred felt very hot and he wanted a rest.

"Here we are!" cried Lord Woodmouse at last.

The baskets were put down and opened, and nettlestem cloths spread out on the mossy grass. In no time at all, the food was unpacked. Wilfred was exhausted. He sat on his basket, too tired to open it, his whiskers drooping sadly.

Mr Apple said grace: "For this good food from our green fields, may we be very grateful."

"I think the knives are in your basket, Wilfred," said Mrs Apple kindly. "If you get them out, we can cut the pies."

Slowly, Wilfred slipped from his perch and undid the catch. When he lifted the lid, he could hardly believe his eyes.

Inside the hamper, packed all around with presents, was an enormous cake, and on the top, written in pink icing, was HAPPY BIRTHDAY WILFRED.

"Happy Birthday, dear Wilfred,
Happy Birthday to you," sang the mice.

When Wilfred had opened all his presents, Basil said,
"Give us a tune," so he bashfully stood up and played
Hickory, Dickory, Dandelion Clock on his new whistle.
Mrs Toadflax nudged him meaningfully when he
had finished.

"Er . . . thank you for all my lovely presents,"
said Wilfred, trying to avoid Mrs Crustybread's eye.
She had caught him firing acorns through
her kitchen window earlier in the day.

"Now for tea," announced Daisy Woodmouse.
The mice sat on the grass and Wilfred handed
round the cake.

When tea was over, the grown-ups snoozed under
the bluebells, while the young mice played hide-and-
seek in the primroses.

At last the sun began to sink behind the Far Woods and a chilly breeze blew over the field. It was time to go home.

When the moon came up that night, Brambly Hedge was silent and still. Every mouse was fast asleep.

THE HIGH HILLS

It was the very end of autumn. The weather was damp and chilly and Wilfred was spending the day inside with the weavers. *Clickety, clack* went the loom, *whirr, whirr* went the spinning wheel. Lily and Flax were in a hurry.

"We must finish in time," said Flax. "We promised Mr Apple."

"What are you making?" asked Wilfred.

"Blankets," replied Lily.

"Who are they for?" said Wilfred.

"They are for the voles in the High Hills," replied Flax. "They have just discovered that the moths have eaten all their quilts and they've no time to make new ones before the cold weather comes. They're too busy gathering stores for winter. We're helping out."

"Can I help too?" asked Wilfred.

"That's kind of you, Wilfred, but not just now," said Lily. "Why don't you find yourself a book to read while I finish spinning this wool?"

Wilfred went over to the bookcase. On a shelf, tucked between volumes on dyestuffs and weaves, he found a thick book called *Daring Explorers of Old Hedge Days*. He settled himself comfortably and began to turn the pages.

"Sir Hogweed Horehound," he read, "determined to conquer the highest peak of the High Hills, for there, he knew, he would discover gold. Alone he set forth, taking in his trusty pack all he needed to survive the rigorous journey. . ."

Wilfred sat entranced. The whirr of the spinning wheel became the swish of eagles' wings, the clatter of the loom, the sound of falling rock, and the drops of rain on the window, jewels from the depths of some forgotten cave. Was there really gold in the hills beyond Brambly Hedge, he wondered.

Suddenly a door slammed. It was his mother come to fetch him home for tea.

"I hope he hasn't been too much trouble," said Mrs Toadflax.

"He has been so quiet, we'd almost forgotten he was here," said Lily. "You can send him down again tomorrow if you like."

Lily and Flax were already hard at work when Wilfred arrived the next morning. He settled down by the window again to read about Sir Hogweed Horehound and his intrepid search for gold.

The morning flew past and by the time Mr Apple arrived to collect Wilfred, Flax and Lily had almost finished the cloth.

"I'm sorry we couldn't match the yellow," said Flax. "We've used the last of Grandpa Blackthorn's lichen and no other dye will do."

"Never mind," said Mr Apple. "It's the blankets they need. We'll take them up to the hills tomorrow."

"The hills," repeated Wilfred. "Are you really going up to the High Hills?"

"Yes," replied Mr Apple. "Why?"

"Can I come?" Wilfred asked desperately. "Please say I can."

"Oh, I don't think so," said Mr Apple. "It's too far. We shall have to stay overnight."

"I'll be very good," urged Wilfred.

Mr Apple relented. "We'll see if your mother agrees," he said. "Come on, young mouse. It's time to go home."

To Wilfred's surprise, his mother did agree.

"It will do him good to be in the open air," she said.
Wilfred rushed upstairs to pack. He knew just what
he would need. Sir Hogweed Horehound had listed
all the essential gear in his book: rope, a whistle, food,
firesticks, cooking pots, a groundsheet and blankets,
a spoon, a water bottle and a first-aid kit.

"And I had better have a special bag for the gold,"
said Wilfred to himself as he gathered everything together.

He went to bed straight after supper. It was a long way
to the High Hills and to get to the Voles' Hole by dusk,
they would have to make an early start.

Next morning, soon after dawn, Flax, Lily and Mr Apple called for Wilfred. They were carrying packs on their backs, full of cloth and blankets, and there was honey and cheese and a pudding for the voles from Mrs Apple. Wilfred hurried down the stairs.

"Whatever have you got there?" asked Flax.

"It's my essential gear," explained Wilfred.

"You won't be needing a cooking pot. I've got some sandwiches," said Mr Apple.

"But I must take everything," said Wilfred. His lip began to quiver. "How can I find gold without my equipment?"

"You'll have to carry it then," said Mr Apple. "We can't manage any more."

The first part of the journey was easy. The four mice went up the hedge, past Crabapple Cottage, the Store Stump and Old Oak Palace. Then they rounded the weavers' cottages and arrived at the bank of the stream. Carefully they picked their way over the stepping stones and clambered up into the buttercup meadow.

Wilfred strode through the grass, occasionally lifting his paw to gaze at the distant peaks. Beyond the bluebell woods he could see the path begin to climb.

Mr Apple looked back. "How's my young explorer?" he said. "Ready for lunch?"

"Oh, please," said Wilfred, easing off his pack with relief.

The mice ate their picnic and enjoyed the late autumn sunshine but soon it was time to go on. All through the afternoon they walked. The path became steeper and steeper, and when they looked behind them, they could see the fields and woods and hedges spread out far below.

By tea-time, it was getting dark and cold, and the hills around were shrouded in mist. At last they saw a tiny light shining from a rock beneath an old hawthorn tree.

"Here we are," said Mr Apple. "Knock on the door, Wilfred, will you?"

An elderly vole opened it a crack. When she saw Mr Apple, she cried, "Pip! Fancy you climbing all this way, and with your bad leg too."

"We couldn't leave you without blankets, now could we," said Mr Apple.

The mice crowded into the cottage and were soon sitting round the fire, drinking hot bilberry soup and resting their weary paws.

For Wilfred, the conversation came and went in drifts and soon he was fast asleep. Someone lifted him gently onto a little bracken bed in the corner and the next thing he knew was the delicious smell of breakfast, sizzling on the range.

Wilfred ate heartily, oatcakes with rowanberry jelly, and listened to the voles describing their hard life in the hills. He was disappointed when Mr Apple announced that it was time to leave.

"Can't we explore a bit first?" he begged.

"Flax and I have to get back to work," said Lily, "but why don't you two follow on later?"

"Well," relented Mr Apple, "there are some fine junipers beyond the crag. . ."

"And Mrs Apple *loves* junipers," said Wilfred quickly, "let's get her some."

So the mice said goodbye to the voles and Mr Apple and Wilfred set off up the path.

Wilfred ran on ahead and was soon round the crag. When Mr Apple caught up with him, Wilfred was half way up a steep face of rock.

"Wilfred!" cried Mr Apple. "Come down."

"Just a minute," shouted Wilfred. "I've found something."

Mr Apple watched as Wilfred pulled himself up onto the narrow ledge and started scraping at the rock and stuffing something in his pocket.

"Look!" cried Wilfred. "Gold!"

"Don't be silly, Wilfred," shouted Mr Apple. "That's not gold. Come down at once."

Wilfred looked over the side. His voice faltered. "I can't," he said. "I'm scared."

Mr Apple was exasperated. "Wait there," he shouted. Slowly he climbed the steep rocks, carefully placing his paws in the clefts of the stones. The ledge was very narrow. "We'll edge along this way. Perhaps the two paths

will meet," he said. "We certainly can't go down the way we came up."

As they walked cautiously along the ledge, an ominous mist began to rise from the valley.

"If only we had some rope," said Mr Apple. "We ought to rope ourselves together."

Wilfred put his paw in his pack and produced the rope! Mr Apple tied it carefully round Wilfred's middle

and then round his own. And it was just as well for a few minutes later they were engulfed in a thick white fog.

"Turn to the rock face, Wilfred, we'll ease our way along, one step at a time."

They went on for a long time, then they took a rest. As they sat on the wet rock, the mist parted for a few seconds, just long enough to show a deep strange valley below.

Mr Apple was worried. He had no idea where they were. It looked as though they would have to spend the night on the mountain. It would be very cold and dark, and all he had in his pocket were two sandwiches the voles had given him for the journey down. His leg was feeling stiff and sore too. What was to be done? He explained the situation to Wilfred.

"It's all my fault," said Wilfred, "I didn't mean us to get lost. I just wanted to find gold like Sir Hogweed."

"Never mind," said Mr Apple. "We must look for somewhere to spend the night."

A short way along the path, the ledge became a little wider. Under an overhang of rock a small cave ran back into the mountainside.

"Look," cried Wilfred, slinging his pack inside. "Base camp!"

Mr Apple sat gingerly on the damp moss at the mouth of the cave. Everything felt damp, his clothes, his whiskers, his handkerchief.

"I wish I'd brought my pipe, we could have made a fire," he sighed. "Never mind, we'll huddle close and try to keep warm."

But Wilfred was busily searching in his pack again. Out came the firesticks and the tinderbox. "I'll see if there's some dry wood at the back of the cave," he said enthusiastically.

"Wilfred," cried Mr Apple in admiration, "you're a real explorer."

Soon they had a cheerful blaze on the ledge outside the cave. Wilfred produced two blankets and the mice wrapped themselves up snugly while their clothes dried in front of the fire. The little kettle was filled from the water bottle and proudly Wilfred set out a feast of bread and cheese and honeycakes.

"You know," said Mr Apple, as he settled back against the rock, "I haven't enjoyed a meal so much for years."

To while away the time, Mr Apple began to tell Wilfred stories of his adventurous youth, and as they talked, the mists gradually cleared and a starry sky spread out above them. All was quiet but for the murmur of a stream which ran through the valley below like a silver ribbon in the moonlight. Warmed by the fire, they became drowsy and soon fell asleep.

The next morning they were woken by the sun shining into the cave.

"It's a beautiful day," called Wilfred, peering over the ledge, "and I can see a path down the mountain."

Mr Apple sat up and stretched his leg. It still hurt. "We'll have to go down slowly, I'm afraid," he said.

"Is it your leg?" said Wilfred. "I can help," and he brought out a jar of comfrey ointment from his first-aid kit.

They packed up and set off down the path. Mr Apple did the best he could but his leg was very painful. He managed to get as far as the stream but then he stopped and sat on a boulder with a sigh. "I can't go any further," he said. "What are we to do?"

The two mice sat in silence and watched the water swirl past the bank.

"Don't worry," said Wilfred, trying to be cheerful. "We'll think of something."

Suddenly he jumped up. "I've got it," he cried excitedly. "We'll *sail* down the stream!" He ran to the bank and with his ice-axe, he hooked out some large sticks that had caught behind a rock in the water. Using his rope to lash them together, he made a raft. "Come on," said Wilfred, "we'll shoot the rapids!"

"Are you sure this is a good idea?" said Mr Apple. "Wherever will we end up?"

"Don't worry," said Wilfred. "It's all going to be all right."

Carefully they climbed onto the raft, Mr Apple let go of the bank and they were off!

They were swept to the middle of the stream as it raced down the mountainside, twisting and turning, sweeping and splashing, careering over rocks and cutting through deep banks.

"My hat," shouted Wilfred. "I've lost my hat."

"Never mind that," cried Mr Apple, "just hold on tight. There's a boulder ahead."

Wilfred gripped the sides of the raft, and somehow they managed to keep the raft, and themselves, afloat.

Down by the stream, Dusty was ferrying a search party of mice over to the buttercup meadows when he suddenly caught sight of a small red hat floating along on the current.

"Look there," he shouted. All the mice peered over the side of the boat.

"It's Wilfred's hat," cried out Mrs Toadflax. "Whatever can have happened to him?"

"Can he swim?" asked Mrs Apple anxiously.

Meanwhile Wilfred and Mr Apple were beginning to enjoy their trip on the river. The ground had levelled out and the pace of the stream had become gentler. They looked about them with interest.

"Wilfred," called Mr Apple, "can you see what I can see? I'm sure that's our willow ahead."

Wilfred stared at the bank. "It is!" he yelled.

"And there's the Old Oak Palace and the hornbeam. This is *our* stream!"

As they rounded the bend, they saw the Brambly Hedge mice climbing out of Dusty's boat. At the very same moment, Mrs Apple looked up and cried, "Look! Look! There they are!"

The mice turned in amazement; the raft was almost abreast of them.

"Quick," shouted Dusty, "catch hold of this rope and I'll haul you to shore."

As the two mice clambered out of the raft and up onto the bank, they all hugged each other.

"Wilfred, you're safe," cried Mrs Toadflax.

"My dear, what has happened to your leg?" said Mrs Apple.

Lord Woodmouse took charge. "Come on, everybody," he said. "Let's get these travellers home and dry, and then we can hear the full story."

The mice made their way along the hedgerow to the hornbeam tree. Soon everybody was sitting round the fire, eating cake and drinking acorn coffee.

"Now tell us exactly what happened," urged Flax.

"Well, it was my fault," explained Wilfred again. "I was looking for gold and I got stuck. Mr Apple had to rescue me and then we got lost. And Mr Apple's leg hurt so much, we had to come back on the raft."

"Did you find any gold?" interrupted Primrose.

"No, only this silly old dust," said Wilfred, pulling the bag out of his pocket. Flax and Lily gasped.

"Wilfred! That's not dust. That's Grandpa Blackthorn's lichen. It's very rare. You *are* clever! Wherever did you find it?"

Primrose ran to fetch some paper and Wilfred proudly drew a map so that they could find the place again.

"And when we go, you shall come with us, Wilfred," promised Lily.

Mr Apple was tired and soon he and Mrs Apple went home to Crabapple Cottage. One by one, the visitors drifted away. It was time for the explorer to go to bed.

Wilfred followed his mother up the stairs.

"What adventures!" she said, washing his face and paws and helping him take off his muddy dungarees.

Wilfred climbed into bed. As his mother tucked him in, he thought of his night beneath the stars and snuggling down under his warm blankets, he was soon fast asleep.

BRAMBLY HEDGE

BRAMBLY HEDGE
ACTIVITY BOOK

As seen on television

JILL BARKLEM

FOUR SEASONS
ACTIVITY BOOK

JILL BARKLEM

FOUR SEASONS
COLOURING BOOK

As seen on television and video

JILL BARKLEM

WINTER STORY
COLOURING BOOK

As seen on television

JILL BARKLEM

SPRING STORY
STICKER BOOK

As seen on television

JILL BARKLEM

WINTER STORY
STICKER BOOK

As seen on television

JILL BARKLEM

SPRING STORY
A BIRTHDAY SURPRISE
FOR WILFRED

SUMMER STORY
POPPY AND DUSTY'S
WEDDING DAY

THE SECRET
STAIRCASE
PRIMROSE FINDS
A LOST KEY

POPPY'S BABIES
POPPY AND DUSTY'S
NEW FAMILY

AUTUMN STORY
PRIMROSE MEETS
THE HARVEST MICE

WINTER STORY
A PARTY IN THE
ICE PALACE

PRIMROSE AND WILFRED
SAIL TO SANDY BAY

THE HIGH HILLS
WILFRED'S MOUNTAIN
ADVENTURE

As seen on television and video

JILL BARKLEM